Room
With a Boo

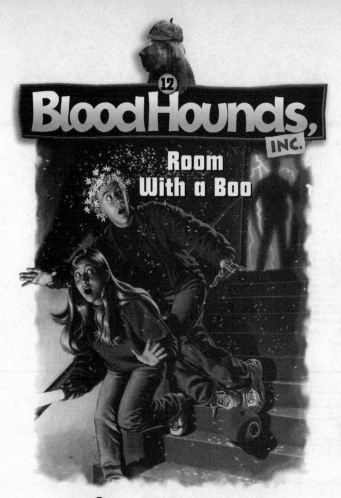

BloodHounds, INC.

12

Room With a Boo

Bill Myers

with DAVE WIMBISH

BETHANY HOUSE PUBLISHERS
MINNEAPOLIS, MINNESOTA 55438

Room With a Boo
Copyright © 2002
Bill Myers

Cover illustration by Joe Nordstrom
Cover design by Lookout Design Group, Inc.

Published by Bethany House Publishers
A Ministry of Bethany Fellowship International
11400 Hampshire Avenue South
Bloomington, Minnesota 55438
www.bethanyhouse.com

Printed in the United States of America by
Bethany Press International, Bloomington, Minnesota 55438

Library of Congress Cataloging-in-Publication Data

Myers, Bill, 1953-
   Room with a boo / by Bill Myers with Dave Wimbish.
      p. cm. — (Bloodhounds, Inc. ; 12)
Summary: With the help of a new invention from Doc, Sean and Melissa win an all-expenses-paid trip to Washington, D.C., where they hope to solve the mystery of a missing helicopter—and of a haunted hotel.
ISBN 0-7642-2624-X (pbk.)
   [1. Spies—Fiction. 2. Brothers and sisters—Fiction. 3. Christian life—Fiction. 4. Mystery and detective stories.] I. Wimbish, David. II. Title.
   PZ7.M98234 Ro   2002
   [Fic]—dc21
                                        2002009662

For Dawson:
Welcome to the family.

BILL MYERS is a youth worker, creative writer, and film director who co-created the "McGee and Me!" book and video series; his work has received over forty national and international awards. His many books include THE INCREDIBLE WORLDS OF WALLY MCDOOGLE series; his teen books: *Hot Topics, Tough Questions; Faith Encounter;* and *Forbidden Doors;* as well as his adult novels: *When the Last Leaf Falls; The Face of God; Eli;* and the trilogy *Blood of Heaven, Threshold,* and *Fire of Heaven.*

Contents

*"You are the light of the world . . .
let your light shine before men,
that they may see your good deeds
and praise your Father in heaven."*

Matthew 5:14, 16

1

The Case Begins

WEDNESDAY, 18:52 PDST

Rafael Ruelas flashed his warmest smile as the cameraman moved in for a close-up. He shuffled through a small stack of papers on his desk, then looked up to the camera and said, "Our next guest on *Midvale Tonight* is Hildagard Tubbs, president of the Midvale Garden Club."

Backstage, the stage manager whispered, "You're on, Mrs. Tubbs." He motioned for her to join Ruelas on the set.

Mrs. Tubbs swallowed hard. In the small mirror posted by the stage entrance she checked her hair to make sure it was still stacked carefully atop her head, examined her overly made-up face (she thought she looked stunning), then walked out to shake Ruelas's hand.

This could be my big moment, she thought. She

smiled as she hoped some big Hollywood producer might see her on TV and think she was perfect to star in the next big movie. Who knew, in the next day or so, she could be hanging out with Brad Pitt.

"Welcome to the show!" Ruelas exclaimed.

Mrs. Tubbs saw him stare at her towering hairdo. *He likes my hair,* she thought. *This is getting off to a great start!* "Thank you, Brad, er, I mean Rafael!" she said.

Ruelas motioned for her to take the seat next to him as the small studio audience, who were sitting on metal folding chairs, applauded politely.

She blinked into the glaring studio lights. She had no idea they were going to be so bright!

Immediately Rafael began to speak. "I understand that you're here to tell us about the Garden Club's annual flower-growing contest."

"That's right, Rafael." *Boy! Those lights are not only bright, they're hot!* She looked around for something to fan herself with. She was getting warmer by the minute.

"Well?" Ruelas asked.

"Well, what?" Mrs. Tubbs answered. At the moment all she could think about was finding a way to keep cool.

"What about the contest?" Ruelas asked as he forced a big, toothy smile.

"Whatcha watchin', sis?" Sean asked. He bounced noisily down the stairs and into the living room.

"Rafael Ruelas's new show," Melissa answered.

"Ruelas has another show?" Sean asked.

Melissa nodded. "I wanted to watch it because he's interviewing Mrs. Tubbs."

"That's Mrs. Tubbs?!" Sean pointed at the television. "Sure doesn't look like her to me."

"I think she's wearing a lot of makeup," Melissa said.

"You can say that again!" Sean agreed. "She must have about a thousand pounds of the stuff on her face."

"Be nice!" Melissa whacked him on the arm.

"Well, it's true. And what's she got on her head, a monkey?"

"Don't be mean," Melissa said. "That's her hair and you know it!"

"Hair?" Sean shook his head. "Nobody has that much hair!"

Melissa fought back a giggle. Her brother was

right. Mrs. Tubbs' hair was a bit much—like Marge Simpson's, except it wasn't blue. The rest of her wasn't that much better. In fact, it looked like she'd been caught in a paint-ball fight. "She just wanted to look pretty on TV," Melissa said.

Sean shook his head. "That's like me trying to convince people I'm as tall as Shaquille O'Neal!"

Now, if you know anything about Bloodhounds, Inc., the detective agency owned by Sean and Melissa, you know that Hildagard Tubbs is their next-door neighbor. She's also what is officially known as a PIN (Pain In the Neck), who always blames the kids, or their huge bloodhound, Slobs, for anything that goes wrong in her neighborhood. (And most of the time she's right.)

"Shhhh!" Melissa hushed her brother. "I want to hear about this contest."

Unfortunately, poor Mrs. Tubbs wasn't saying much of anything. She just sat there, waving herself with her hand.

"And so I understand," Rafael said, "that the Midvale resident who has grown the biggest flower this year will receive an all-expenses-paid trip to Washington, D.C., for two. Is that right, Mrs. Tubbs?"

"What? Washington? Oh yes, that's right."

"And you will be doing the judging?"

Suddenly Mrs. Tubbs seemed to remember why she was there. "Yes, our judges will be walking around Midvale over the next few days, and we'll make our decision within a week."

Ruelas quickly extended his hand. Apparently he'd had enough. "Why, thank you, Hildagard Tubbs. You've certainly been an exciting guest. And now—" He abruptly drew back his hand, and his mouth flew open. It looked as if he'd seen something terrible. "Why, Mrs. Tubbs!" he sputtered. "I do believe you're melting!"

And she was! Well, at least her makeup was!

Her forehead seemed to be sliding down over her eyes, and her mascara oozed down her face, leaving muddy tracks behind. She looked like the Wicked Witch of the West, from *The Wizard of Oz*, after Dorothy hit her with the water.

She clasped her hands to her face, trying to push everything back into place. But when she pulled them away, a big glob of her face stuck to them.

The cameraman tried to avoid this unpleasant scene by swinging his camera in the direction of the studio audience. Unfortunately, the people were stampeding over each other trying to get out of the building.

"She's turning into a monster!" someone shouted.

"We've got to get out of here!" another screamed.

13

KERASH! BOOM!

An entire row of chairs fell backward to the floor.

The cameraman swung his camera back toward Mrs. Tubbs, who was also trying to run out of the studio. But her eyes were so covered with dripping makeup that she couldn't see where she was going.

KA-BANG!

"Ow!" She bounced off the post supporting one of the studio lights, which . . .

KER-THUNK!

. . . crashed down upon her head and . . .

SSSSSSSSSSSSS

. . . smoke, or maybe it was steam, curled out of Mrs. Tubbs' hair.

(She was right about those lights. They *were* hot!)

Immediately a message filled the TV screen:

> **"Please stand by.**
> **We are experiencing technical difficulties."**

Melissa punched Off on the remote control, and the screen went dark. "Poor Mrs. Tubbs," she groaned.

"Well, at least she can't blame us this time," Sean said. Then, changing the subject, he asked, "So, you about ready to go?"

"Go?" Melissa glanced at her watch. "Oh great! It's later than I thought!"

"Don't tell me you forgot about Youth Group?"

"No, I didn't forget," Melissa answered. "I'll just need a minute to comb my hair and . . ." Her voice trailed off as she ran up the stairs to the bathroom.

Sean sighed and clicked the TV back on. When Melissa said she needed a minute to comb her hair, it would mean another hour before you'd see her again.

Girls . . . go figure.

WEDNESDAY, 19:23 PDST

This time it only took twenty-three minutes.

When Melissa came back downstairs, she was surprised to find her brother watching the news instead of cartoons. The reporter talked about a ring of international spies in Washington, D.C., that had been stealing government secrets. Sean was definitely intrigued, especially when it got to the part about them stealing a top secret helicopter called the *Dragonfly*. No one knew where it had gone, though they suspected that it was still somewhere in the city.

Later, as the young detectives walked along Fourth

Street on their way to the church building, Sean was deep in thought.

"Stop it," Melissa said. "You're scaring me."

"Stop what?" Sean asked.

"Thinking!" she replied.

"Stop thinking?" Sean repeated.

"Yeah. You're not used to it, and your brain might explode."

"Very funny. Ha ha!"

"What are you thinking about, anyway?" she asked.

"That Garden Club contest Mrs. Tubbs was talking about."

"What about it?" Melissa asked.

"I was wondering if we had a chance to win it."

"You've got to be kidding!" Melissa laughed. "Have you taken a look at the flowers in front of our house?"

"We have flowers?"

"We did till I killed them," Melissa said. "I have what's known as a brown thumb. I touch plants and they die! Besides, why would you want to win a flower-growing contest anyway?"

"Because then we'd get to go to Washington, D.C. And if we did, I bet we could catch those spies!"

Melissa shook her head. "We're never going to get

there on my flowers." She gave her brother a playful punch on the arm.

"Ow!" he cried. "You scratched me."

"Sorry."

"Well, be careful with that ring, will you?" Sean pouted.

Melissa looked down at the new ring her dad had just bought her. She loved it! It was red, white, and blue and spelled out U.S.A in rhinestones. But Sean was right, some of those stones were kind of sharp.

"Hey, did you forget your Bible again?" she suddenly asked.

"Forget it? No, I've got it right here."

"Here *where*?"

Sean pulled up his shirt to reveal his Bible tucked into the waistband of his pants.

"What are you doing that for?" Melissa asked.

Sean shrugged. "No reason."

"Are you trying to hide it?" Melissa asked.

Sean didn't answer.

"Sean! Are you embarrassed about being a Christian?"

"Look! It's no big deal. It's just not cool to walk around carrying a Bible, all right? It's kind of . . . geeky."

Melissa said nothing. But it had been happening

17

more and more often—as if Sean thought being a Christian meant being a loser.

WEDNESDAY, 21:15 PDST

"You're not still mad at me, are you?" Sean asked as they headed home from youth group.

"Mad? Why should I be mad?" Melissa answered. "Just because you were acting like some undercover Christian on the way to youth group, then some Holy Joe, superChristian during it?"

"I wasn't acting," Sean protested. "I was just being myself."

"Which time?" Melissa asked. "In church, or out?"

Sean had no answer.

"Well, you'd better hide that Bible again," Melissa huffed. "You wouldn't want anyone out here to think you're a Christian."

"Look," Sean said as he raced to keep up with her, "I'm sorry about that. Just forget it, okay?"

"It's already forgotten," Melissa replied. But she didn't slow down.

The kids were around the corner from Doc's, and that gave Sean an idea. Maybe if they stopped by for a little visit, Melissa would get out of her rotten mood.

"Hey!" he said. "You wanna drop in and see what Doc's up to?"

Melissa looked at her watch. "It's kind of late, isn't it?"

"It's only 9:15. Dad won't even be home yet."

It was true. Dad's radio station, KRZY, was in the process of increasing its power to 5,000 watts, and that meant he was rarely home before 10 P.M. these days.

"Well," Melissa said, "maybe we could stop by for a few minutes."

They turned the corner and headed up the sidewalk to Doc's front door. It was always fun at her house. She was a brilliant inventor, and you never knew what amazing invention she might be working on. Sean and Melissa were still about ten feet away from the door when Doc appeared. She swung it open and gestured for them to come inside.

How did you know we were coming? Melissa used sign language to talk to their deaf friend.

Doc pointed to her eyes.

"She has new glasses," Sean said.

"But that still doesn't explain how she saw us through the door," Melissa replied.

Doc, who is great at reading lips, handed the

glasses to Melissa. She motioned for her to put them on.

"Hey, cool!" Melissa shouted. "I can see right through the wall!"

"X-ray glasses!" Sean exclaimed. "Let me try 'em on."

New and improved X-ray glasses, Doc signed. She grabbed a nearby clipboard and wrote:

I've improved the old ones by increasing the subatomic beta frequency and bombarding it with anti-nucleonic beams. So, as you can imagine, they are completely safe.

"Wow!" Sean exclaimed as he stepped outside. "What a view!" He wandered back down the sidewalk toward the street, *ooh*ing and *ahh*ing at everything he saw along the way.

"Sean, be careful," Melissa called after him. "You remember what happened when you tried on the older pair of X-ray glasses?"

He didn't answer.

"Well, I do!" she shouted after him. "Who could ever forget something like that?"

(If you have, you can review the entire case in *Phantom of the Haunted Church*.)

Melissa turned to Doc. "Are you sure you want to do this?" she asked.

Doc smiled. *Like I said, they're perfectly safe,* she signed. *And you'd be doing me a favor if you tried them out for a while.*

"Okay," Melissa said as she slipped her glasses into the pocket of her sweater. "But I hope we both don't regret this." She turned to see what her brother was up to.

"Sean!" she screamed. "Get out of the way!"

He stood in the middle of the street as a big station wagon raced toward him, about to turn him into a giant Sean-sized grease spot.

"Sean! Move!"

But he didn't budge. He stood as if paralyzed, staring at the car that was about to make him an ex-detective!

It was forty feet away!

"Seeeaaannnnn!"

Thirty . . .

"Mooove!"

Twenty . . . ten . . .

Melissa covered her eyes with her hands. She couldn't bear to look!

2

"Look Out, D.C., Here We Come!"

Melissa grimaced at the sound of the car's tires screeching on pavement.

EEEEEEEEE . . .

"Hey! Get out of the road!"

She opened her eyes. The station wagon disappeared down the road as the driver, a little old lady, shook her fist in Sean's direction. Skid marks showed that the driver had just barely managed to swerve around her brother.

Melissa ran into the street, planning to give him a big hug . . . until she became angry over him being so foolish. So instead of embracing him, she . . .

WHOOMP!

. . . stiff-armed him right in the chest.

"Ooooof!" Sean staggered backward and fell hard onto his rear.

"What was that for?" he cried.

"You could've been killed!" Melissa shouted.

"So you're going to beat me up 'cause I wasn't?" Sean asked as he slowly got to his feet.

"I just don't know how you can be so stupid sometimes!"

"But it was cool!" Sean said. He smiled as he rubbed the dirt from the seat of his pants. "I could see inside the engine, and the people in the car looked like skeletons! I just couldn't take my eyes off of it!"

"That does it!" Melissa said. "Give me those glasses right now before you hurt yourself!"

"Not on your life!"

"Sean!"

"No way!"

"Give them to me!"

"Forget it! I'm wearing these babies as much as possible!"

THURSDAY, 7:14 PDST

The morning light poured in. Sean glanced at the clock, then pulled the covers over his head. "Please, be quiet!" he moaned.

He'd crawled into bed just a few hours earlier. Before that, he'd been sitting out in the yard, looking at his sister's petunias in the moonlight. Those flowers may not have been much to look at with the naked eye, but when you saw them through Doc's X-ray glasses—well, they were truly amazing! Who would have guessed there were so many intricate little parts in there? All of them working together to keep the flower healthy and help it grow.

Sean hadn't meant to stay up so late, but he figured it was okay, because this was a "teacher's workday," which meant he didn't have to go to school. He snuggled farther down under the covers, still trying to drown out the noise. His plan had been to sleep in as late as possible. But how could anybody sleep with all that commotion going on?

He sighed in exasperation, threw back the covers, and marched over to his bedroom door.

Melissa, still in her pajamas, stood at the top of the stairs.

"What's going on out there?" she yawned.

"Beats me," he replied. "But whoever it is, I'm going to give them a piece of my mind!"

Melissa followed him downstairs to the door. As they got closer, they could hear their father's voice coming from the front yard.

"I have no idea how they did it," he said. "You'll have to ask them."

"Well, where are they?" someone asked. His voice sounded strangely familiar.

"I hope they're upstairs still aslee—" But before Dad could finish his sentence, Sean opened the door.

"Here they are!" someone shouted.

Video lights came on, and the crowd that had gathered in the Hunters' front yard cheered wildly.

An arm thrust a microphone in Sean's face.

"Tell me, kids, how in the world did you ever grow flowers like these! They're magnificent!"

When Sean's eyes finally recovered from the explosion of light, he could see that the arm with the microphone was attached to . . . Rafael Ruelas!

"What flowers are you talking about?" Sean asked. "We didn't do—"

"Sean, look!" Melissa gasped and pointed toward their father. Something leafy and colorful towered over his head. It was a gigantic petunia!

Her flowers, which had looked so weak and sickly

the night before, had gotten well in a hurry.

Well?! That was an understatement. They had become the Arnold Schwarzenegger of petunias!

In one night, they had shot up six feet. Their petals measured two or three feet across.

As Sean and Melissa stood with their mouths hanging open, Mrs. Tubbs made her way out of the crowd. Her own mouth was twisted into a sneer. She meant it to be a smile, but it wasn't quite working out that way.

"Congratulations," she said, but she didn't really sound like she meant it. She handed them a brass plaque. "You won first prize. You're going to Washington, D.C."

SATURDAY, 20:13 CDST

Snzzzzz! Woooo! Snzzzzzz!

"I've never heard anybody snore that loud!" Sean whispered to Melissa, who sat across the aisle of the bus from him.

Melissa nodded as she continued playing her computer game.

Sean sighed and gently tried to move Mrs. Tubbs,

who was sitting beside him, to the other side of her seat. It was no use. Her head fell back across his shoulder, and her snoring grew louder.

SNZZZZZZ! WOOO! SNZZZZZZ!

"I'm not sure I would've wanted first prize if I'd known she was going along as our chaperone," Sean grumbled.

"Or that we were going to have to spend seventeen straight hours riding on a bus," Melissa agreed. "I wonder where we are right now?"

Sean pulled the bus schedule out of his pocket and studied it. "I think we're somewhere in the middle of Tennessee," he said. "Or maybe it's Minnesota. I can't tell for sure."

Mrs. Tubbs had stopped snoring for a moment. Now she was babbling in her sleep. "Candy? For me? Oh, Brad, you're so romantic!"

"At least she's having a good time," Melissa laughed. She leaned forward to get a better look at her brother. "What's that in your hair?" she asked.

"I don't know," he replied. "What does it look like?"

"Grass," she said.

Sean shrugged. "Probably just something the wind blew in."

He pulled his comb out of his pocket and ran it through his hair. "There. That ought to take care of it."

Back in the baggage compartment, the kids' huge bloodhound, Slobs, lay patiently in her kennel. A little puddle of drool had collected on the floor in front of her, and a tiny river of the stuff trickled out of her cage and onto the bus floor.

Slobs, as you may know by now, was short for Slobbers, which was something she did a lot of. Something else she did a lot of was tracking criminals. That was why Sean had insisted the garden club let him and Melissa bring her to the nation's capital. With her help, they just might be able to find that missing helicopter.

In the kennel next to Slobs slept Mrs. Tubbs' fat cat, Precious. He looked like he had a smile on his face while he was sleeping, probably dreaming about turning into a lion and chasing all the dogs, including Slobs, out of his neighborhood.

Slobs might have been asleep, too, but who could fall asleep with that cat . . .

snzzz . . . wooo . . . snzzz!

. . . snoring away like that?

Mrs. Tubbs' dream date with Brad Pitt was apparently over and she, too, had gone back to . . .

SNZZZZ! WOOO! SNZZZZing!

Sean sighed, fished his Walkman out of his bag, and put his earphones on. Maybe he could find some good music on the radio to drown out that awful racket. But instead of music, he tuned in to the news:

"And still no word on the location of the Navy's supersonic helicopter, the Dragonfly, *or of the spies who have stolen it. An angry President George Shrub met with his closest advisors today and demanded that everything possible be done to arrest the perpetrators and bring them to justice."*

"Don't worry, Mr. President," Sean said to himself. "We'll catch those spies for you!"

"Level five! All right! I finally made it!" Melissa shouted. "Woo-hoo!"

She thrust her handheld videogame, *Spy Guys,* across the aisle and into her brother's face. Sean's record, which had lasted for three months, had fallen.

In her excitement, she shouted, "And the new champion is. . . !"

Sean, of course, had his earphones on, so he couldn't hear her. But the sudden movement in front of his face startled him.

"Whazzat!" He brought his hands up to protect himself and . . .

WHACK!

. . . hit the videogame hard enough to send it flying. It bounced off the ceiling and clattered to the floor.

Unfortunately, at that very moment, the bus was passing the biggest electrical power plant in the entire state of Tennessee . . . or was it Minnesota? Suddenly the videogame . . .

SSSSed
and
POP! POP! POPed

Melissa cried, "What's going on with my . . ."

SHAZAM!

A bright flash of light shot through the bus. Suddenly a glowing green "monster" stood in front, facing the passengers. (Actually, he looked more like a leprechaun than a monster, and he seemed just as surprised to be there as the passengers.)

"Jeremiah!" Sean and Melissa yelled at the same time.

31

Everybody else on the bus was yelling, too. But they weren't yelling anyone's name. They were just yelling. All except Mrs. Tubbs, who was still . . .

SNZZZS! WOOO! SNSZZZing!

Now, just in case you didn't already know, Jeremiah stands for *Johnson Electronic Reductive Entity Memory Inductive Assembly Housing.* He is one of Doc's first, best, and most troublesome inventions. He is also a creature made up entirely of electrical energy. Being made of electricity, Jeremiah can go anywhere there's electrical current. He spends most of his time hanging out in Sean's digital watch or in Melissa's computer game. But when conditions are just right—or wrong, depending on your point of view—he can even appear in the "real" world. Sean and Melissa never know where he's going to show up next, and sometimes neither does he!

Jeremiah seemed to be thinking up something to say. Finally he opened his mouth. "I want to hurt you!" he shouted over the screaming, which grew even louder. Passengers scrambled over each other in their hurry to get to the back of the bus—and away from the scary green, er, whatever-it-was.

"Did you hear that?" shouted an elderly lady with blue hair. "He said he wants to hurt us! Aaaaagggh!"

Of course, what Jeremiah really meant to say was, "I *won't* hurt you," but like everything else he said, it came out wrong. (Did I mention that he was involved in an explosion in a fortune-cookie factory? Ever since then, he's recited mixed-up proverbs and he's had trouble getting his words right.)

"I'm pleased to meet you!" Jeremiah shouted. (At least that's what he meant to shout. What he actually said was, "I'm pleased to *eat* you!")

The comment brought even more screaming!

Melissa grabbed her brother's elbow. "Sean," she cried, "who's driving this bus?"

"The driver?"

"Oh yeah? Well, then, who's that lying on the floor?"

"Oh no!" Sean yelled. "The driver's fainted! Jeremiah, do something!"

But when Jeremiah saw the driver lying unconscious on the floor, he did the only sensible thing he could do. . . .

He fainted, too!

Sparks shot off of him as he collapsed to the floor in a glowing green heap. Then, with a buzzing sound, he disappeared, transported back to the world of amps and kilowatts. Unfortunately, there was still the little problem with the bus. It hit the . . .

THWACK!

. . . guardrail on the right-hand side of the road and began drifting back to the left where it . . .

K-WHACK!

. . . hit the other side!

Sean and Melissa staggered back and forth, trying to fight their way to the front so they could grab the steering wheel, until the bus . . .

KER-UNCH!

. . . crashed right through the guardrail!

The impact sent Sean and Melissa tumbling to the floor.

And it woke Mrs. Tubbs, who immediately began screaming, "Somebody stop them! They're trying to kill us all!" She pushed a window open and frantically tried to climb out. But it was no use. The bus was moving too fast for her to jump. She'd just have to come back inside and take her chances.

That's when she made another terrifying discovery.

She couldn't get back inside! She was stuck halfway out the window!

The bus shot off the highway and bounced into a cornfield at sixty miles per hour.

Sean made a flying leap for the steering wheel . . .

WHOOOMP!

"Ow!" And just missed.

WHAP! WHAP! WHAP!

Stalks of corn slapped against the bus . . . and Mrs. Tubbs.

"Ow! Ow! Ow!" she yelled as hard ears of unripe corn played bongo drums on her head and shoulders, until the bus . . .

KER-WHACK!

. . . smashed through a wall and into a barn, where a farmer was hard at work milking a cow.

Sean pulled himself into the driver's seat just in time to see the panicked look on the farmer's face.

HONK! HONK!

The man dropped his pail and jumped out of the way just in time as . . .

MOOOOOO!

. . . the frightened cow kicked the pail high into the air. It seemed to hang there for a long moment. Then it slowly began to turn as it fell down . . . down . . . down . . . and finally . . .

KER-SPLAT!

. . . landed upside down on Mrs. Tubbs' head.

Milk ran down her face, dripped from her ears, and soaked her official Midvale Garden Club blouse. Finally she freed herself from the pail just as Sean stomped on the brakes.

EEEEEEEEEEE!

The tires locked as the big vehicle kicked up a cloud of dust, skidding through the barnyard.

"Noooooooo!" Mrs. Tubbs screamed. Dust stuck to her wet face and hair. "What else can happen to me?" she cried.

She was about to find out!

Melissa had managed to get to her feet and was standing by Sean, trying to help him steer. But it was no use. There was no way to avoid . . .

KER-SMASH!

. . . that fence just ahead.

"Look!" Melissa shouted and pointed. "We've got to stop! Now!"

A canyon with a sheer drop lay straight ahead. If the bus went over the cliff, that would probably be the end of everyone on board.

"I'm doing everything I can!" Sean shouted.

"Turn the wheel!" Melissa shouted.

"It won't turn!" Sean shouted back.

The cliff was fifty yards away and approaching fast. As far as everyone could tell, it looked like Bloodhounds, Inc., was about to go out with a bang!

3

"You Ghosts Be Quiet! We're Trying to Sleep Here!"

Death was forty yards away and closing fast!

"We're slowing down!" Sean shouted.

"But we're still going too fast!" Melissa yelled back. "We've got to turn the steering wheel!"

She grabbed hold of the wheel and again tried to help Sean turn it, but it was still no use.

Suddenly the kids felt another pair of hands on the wheel.

The driver had regained consciousness!

The three of them twisted the steering wheel to the right as hard as they could.

ERRRRR! EEEEEE!

Somehow, at the very edge of that canyon, the bus turned.

Its tires screamed.

Its engine rattled and coughed.

And the big vehicle shuddered to a stop on the very edge of the yawning chasm.

Unfortunately . . .

"Yiiiiiiiiiii!"

. . . the sudden change of direction, coupled with the skidding stop, caused Mrs. Tubbs to shoot out of the vehicle.

Up, up, up she went!

Out, out, out over the cliff!

And down, down, down into the canyon!

Melissa grabbed her brother's arm. "Oh no!" she shrieked.

Everyone else in the bus was catching their breath or regaining consciousness.

The two kids scrambled outside and ran to the edge of the cliff. When they got there, Melissa couldn't bear to look. "Is she . . . is she dead?" she moaned.

"Hardly!" Sean replied. "Look!"

Melissa opened her eyes and saw that Mrs. Tubbs had landed safely in a lake. At the moment, she was dog-paddling her way back to shore.

"You see," Sean smiled at his sister. "Everything always works out."

"How in the world can you possibly say that?" Melissa demanded.

"Simple," he said. "After that trip through the barnyard, Mrs. Tubbs needed a bath. And now she's getting one!"

SUNDAY, 21:13 EDST

Sean was thrilled. "I can't believe we're really here!" he said.

"Me neither," Melissa yawned. "I need some sleep."

"But aren't you excited to be in this hotel?" Sean asked. "I mean, Abraham Lincoln stayed here! So did Ulysses S. Grant . . . and Robert E. Lee! This place has so much history!"

Melissa yawned again. "All I care is that it has a bed. I haven't slept for thirty-six hours, and I'm exhausted!" She pulled back the covers on the bed next to the window and crawled in. "In fact," she said, "I'm so tired that I'm not even going to wash up."

BALOOOOO!

Melissa sat up and looked at her brother. "I told

you not to eat all those burritos," she said. "How many was it? Twelve?"

Sean shook his head in protest. "That wasn't my stomach," he said.

"Then what. . . ?"

BALOOOOOOOOOOO!

There it was again—a strange moaning sound, just a little bit louder and longer than before.

Sean put his ear to the wall. "I think it's coming from in there," he said.

"Great!" Melissa exclaimed. "I wonder how many burritos Mrs. Tubbs had." She pulled the covers up over her head. "I've just gotta get some sleep!"

WOOOOOAAAAAA!

"That's not Mrs. Tubbs' room," Sean said. "She's on the other side of us. And it can't be Slobs howling. She's downstairs in the kennel."

"HA! HA! HA! HAAAAAAAAA!"

"Well, whoever it is, I'm going to go right over there and tell them to keep it down," Melissa pouted.

The laughing abruptly stopped. Everything grew quiet. Then the moaning started again.

Melissa threw back her covers and jumped out of bed.

"That does it!" she said. "Where are those X-ray glasses? I want to see what's going on in that room."

"But you can't invade someone's privacy like that," Sean argued.

"Why not? They've already invaded mine. Ah, here they are!" She fished the glasses out of her handbag, put them on, and faced the wall.

WOOOOAAAAAAA!

Melissa just stood there without saying a word.

"What?" Sean asked. "What do you see?"

When she didn't answer, he said, "Oh, never mind. I'll see for myself." He found his glasses, put them on, and looked through the wall.

The room was empty. Totally and completely empty.

SUNDAY, 22:09 EDST

The hotel's night manager peered over his glasses.

"What seems to be the problem?" he asked.

"The problem is that we've got to get some sleep," Melissa huffed.

"Strange noises are coming from the room next door," Sean explained.

43

The night manager pushed his glasses back up on his nose. "What kind of noises?" he asked.

"Someone moaning and wailing," Melissa said.

"Your room number, please," the man asked.

"Five-seventy-two," Sean answered.

"That means you're right next to 570." The man sighed and nodded. "I thought so. I'm going to move you to another room."

"Why?" Sean asked. "What's going on in there?"

"I don't know."

"What do you mean you don't know?" Melissa challenged.

The night manager sighed again. "Well, some people think that room is haunted."

"Haunted?" Sean and Melissa both said the word at the same time.

"By who?" Melissa asked.

"Union soldiers," the man said.

"From the Civil War?!" Sean exclaimed.

"That's right," the man nodded. "Not that I believe it. There's bound to be a natural explanation. A regiment of the Fifth Cavalry was headquartered here for a while in 1863. Ever since those days, there's been a legend that the hotel is haunted. Only recently . . ." his voice trailed off.

"Recently what?" Melissa asked.

44

"It seems to be getting worse."

"Worse?" Sean repeated. "How?"

"Over the past several months we've had a lot of people say they've seen ghostly soldiers wandering the halls. Others have heard noises. Moaning, laughing, crying, the sound of horse hooves galloping past. And most of it seems connected to room 570."

"Wow!" Sean exclaimed.

"Yes, well, anyway," the night manager said, smiling, "I'm going to move you down to room 326."

Sean took the new room key, and he and his sister hurried back to their old room to retrieve their suitcases.

"Imagine that! We're staying in a haunted hotel!"

"It's not haunted," Melissa said. "You know there's no such thing as a ghost."

"Oh yeah," Sean gulped. Then, with a shaking hand, he pointed, "Then what's that?"

Just ahead of them, in the dim light of the hall, stood a man dressed in the unmistakable blue uniform of the Union Army. The brass buttons and buckles gleamed in the light. His hand rested on the sword that hung at his side. He wore a long, gray beard, and his skin was just as gray. He had a thin, crooked nose, which looked as if it had been broken at one time. His bushy eyebrows ran in one straight line across his forehead, and his eyes stared straight ahead, as if he didn't see Sean and Melissa.

Melissa grabbed her brother's arm.

"Sean," she whispered, "he's coming straight at us!"

4

Ring Around the Rose Garden

The ghostly soldier was almost upon them, his hand still resting upon his sword. He was within a few feet when Sean suddenly grabbed his sister's arm and pulled her out of the way. They stood with their backs pressed against the wall as the "ghost" strode past. His eyes never seemed to acknowledge their presence.

They turned and watched him march down the hall. He had disappeared around a corner by the time Melissa caught her breath enough to say, "He didn't look like a ghost to me."

"How do you know?" Sean asked. "You ever seen a ghost before?"

Melissa put her hands on her hips. "How could I

ever see something that doesn't exist?" she asked. "He just looked . . . too solid."

"Come on," Sean said. "Let's follow him and see where he went!"

Melissa forgot about how tired she was as she and her brother ran down the hall to catch the "ghost." But when they rounded the corner, no one was there.

"He's gone!" she exclaimed.

"But where'd he go?" Sean asked.

Melissa pointed at the door marked Exit. "Maybe he went down the stairs."

"Good thinking," Sean replied. "Let's go."

The two young detectives raced down the stairs, all the way to the first floor, without seeing anything unusual. But when they reached the door that led out to the street, it was left standing open, as if someone had just gone through it. Sean and Melissa ran outside. Even at this late hour, the street was crowded with tourists.

"We'll never find him out here," Melissa complained. "We might as well go back to our room."

"Yeah, I guess you're right," Sean agreed.

They turned back toward their hotel when a tall man, wrapped in an overcoat, stepped out of the shadows and stood in front of them. Without saying a word, he thrust something at them.

"Look out!" Sean shouted. "He's got a knife!" He pushed the man, making him stumble, as he and Melissa took off back to the hotel.

The man quickly regained his balance and started after them shouting, "Hey! This is for you!"

He quickly gained on them until . . .

"Augh!" Sean cried as he hit a pothole and fell face-down.

Melissa ran back to help, but she was too late. The man with the knife was upon them. "Here!" he said. "Take this!" He jabbed at them with his . . .

"Wait a minute!" Melissa shouted. "That's not a knife. It's a—"

"Tract," the man finished her sentence. "It tells how you can be born again."

"Born again!" Sean shouted as he rose and dusted himself off. "You scared us half to death!"

"Don't you want to know about Jesus, God's Son?" the man asked.

"Is this fellow bothering you?" someone asked. The voice belonged to a uniformed security guard from the hotel.

"I was just trying to tell them about Jesus," the man protested.

"I've told you to quit pestering people out here," the security guard snapped.

"He wasn't pestering—" Melissa started.

"Nobody wants to hear about Jesus tonight," the security guard said. "So beat it!"

Melissa looked at Sean, expecting him to say something in the man's defense, but he didn't open his mouth.

As for the fellow in the overcoat, he looked big enough to snap the security guard in two. But he didn't even get angry. Instead, he just said "All right" as he tucked his tract back into his pocket. "But don't forget: Jesus loves you." With that, he turned away and headed back into the darkness.

Sean shook his head as he watched him go. "What a geek!" he said.

"At least he's not ashamed of his faith," Melissa countered.

"Oh yeah!" Sean shot back. "Is that what you want me to be like? Well, no thanks!"

MONDAY, 7:23 EDST

When Melissa woke up the next morning, Sean was already gone. That was unusual, to say the least. If there was anything Sean liked more than eating, it was sleeping in. Nevertheless, Melissa found him in the hotel lobby.

"What are you doing up so early?" she asked.

"I didn't get a whole lot of sleep," he said. "I guess I was kind of . . . I don't know . . . feeling guilty."

"Guilty?" Melissa asked.

"Yeah, I should have defended that guy last night. Or at least let him know I was a Christian, too."

Melissa agreed, not letting him off the hook. "You're right. Lately, it's like you're embarrassed to be a Christian or something."

Sean sighed. "Yeah." Then, changing the subject, he said, "Anyway, I've been watching that guy over there. I think he's up to something." He nodded his head in the direction of a man sitting in an overstuffed chair, chatting on a cell phone.

"Why?" Melissa whispered. "What's he doing?"

"Wait until he puts the phone down," Sean whispered. "Then take a look at his mustache."

Melissa didn't have long to wait.

"Yes, dear, I'll be home tomorrow," the man was saying. "I love you, too. Kiss-kiss!" He said it too loud, as if he wanted people to think he was talking to his wife when he was really talking to someone else. He clicked the phone off and dropped it into his briefcase. Now Melissa could clearly see his face.

"He only has half a mustache!" she exclaimed.

"That's because I have the other half right here!" Sean opened his hand to reveal something that resembled a fuzzy caterpillar.

"How did you. . . ?" Melissa began.

"I was in the elevator with him when it fell off," he said. "Obviously he's wearing a disguise. I'll bet he's one of those spies we've been hearing about."

Melissa thought for a moment. "Or maybe he just thinks he looks better with a mustache."

"Yeah, well, just before you got here, I saw him talking to his ball-point pen," Sean said.

"Doing *what*?" Melissa asked, wondering if her brother's imagination had been working overtime again.

"That's right," Sean said, "talking to his pen. He took it out of his pocket, clicked it, and started talking into it. I'm not kidding. There's something very strange about this guy, and we'd better keep—"

"Oh, there you are!"

Sean and Melissa both wheeled around and looked into the smiling face of Mrs. Tubbs.

"I've been looking for you," the woman said sweetly. "We don't want to be late now, do we?"

Melissa glanced at her watch. "Oh, that's right!"

she said. "We've got a tour of the White House this morning."

"Better than that," gushed Mrs. Tubbs. "We're going to attend a ceremony in the White House Rose Garden. President Shrub is going to be there."

"He is?" Sean asked.

"Yes. He's going to be accepting a special gift from the Royal Family of Who-kares-ik-stan. Who knows? We might even get to meet him."

"Cool!" Sean exclaimed. He turned to his sister. "Do I look okay?" he asked.

"Now, there's a switch," Melissa laughed. "You worrying about how you look."

"It's not every day you get a chance to meet the president," Sean replied.

"Well, you look fine, except—" Melissa stopped in mid-sentence and reached up to pull something out of Sean's hair. "You have some more of that grass—or whatever it is—in your hair."

Sean shrugged. "It's probably pollen," he said. "I can tell there's a lot of it in the air. AH-CHOOO! See what I mean? Oh, sorry, Mrs. Tubbs," he said. "I didn't mean to sneeze all over you."

"That's all right, dear." She pulled a handkerchief from her purse and dabbed at her face.

Sean and Melissa exchanged nervous glances.

Could Mrs. Tubbs be acting any weirder? She acted so . . . so . . . well, almost . . . nice. Not like herself at all.

"Just think how grand it's going to be," she said. "A president—that's me," she clasped her hands together, "gets to meet another president—Mr. Shrub."

"You're a president?" Sean asked.

"Of the Midvale Garden Club," Mrs. Tubbs snapped angrily, but then she quickly became sweet again. "You know that, dear," she smiled.

"Of course, Mrs. Tubbs, I just forgot," Sean apologized.

"Can Slobs go with us?" Melissa asked.

"Slobs? Well, I'm not sure if they allow dogs . . ."

"We'd hate to keep her locked up inside all day," Sean said. "And what about Precious? Wouldn't he like to meet the president?"

Mrs. Tubbs threw her hands into the air. "Oh, why not. They'll have fun. But remember," she shook her finger at Sean, "that dog of yours better be on her leash."

"All the time," Sean promised. "All the time!"

MONDAY, 11:17 EDST

The White House Rose Garden was gorgeous—like a huge rainbow full of flowers of every imaginable color, including a few Melissa had never seen before.

The kids waited nervously, along with a few congressmen and some other dignitaries, for the president to arrive. Slobs, on her leash, sat obediently at their feet. It was almost as if she knew something special was going on and that she was expected to be on her best behavior.

Not far away, Mrs. Tubbs, with Precious on his rhinestone-studded leash, was talking . . . and talking . . . and talking some more to a tall, distinguished-looking man with salt-and-pepper hair. Melissa giggled as she saw the man looking for a way of escape.

But Mrs. Tubbs didn't notice at all. She just kept on . . . you guessed it, talking.

"We should've brought another leash," Melissa whispered to her brother, gesturing in Mrs. Tubbs' direction.

"It wouldn't have helped," Sean said.

"Oh yes," Mrs. Tubbs was saying, "I've been friends with the president for years. Every time he has an important decision to make, he calls to ask for my advice."

"You—" The man tried to speak, but Mrs. Tubbs' verbal steamroller stopped him after one word:

"I'm a president, too, you know. That's right. Of the Midvale Garden Club. You've probably heard of it. It's one of the best and biggest garden clubs in the entire tri-state area."

"I'm sure—" he tried again.

"So, of course, Precious and I come to the White House all the time," she said. "How about you? Do you come here often? I mean, I'd be happy to give you a tour later on. President Shrub won't mind, I'm sure. Like I said, we're old friends and—"

"Oh, there you are, Mr. Vice-President! I've been looking for you." The voice belonged to a pleasant-looking blond woman, who wore an elegant blue pantsuit.

"Hi, Donna," the man said. Then, turning to Mrs. Tubbs, he explained, "Donna is my press secretary, and this is, uh . . . you know, I don't think I got your name."

"Hildagard Tubbs," she sniffed.

"Pleased to meet you, Ms. Tubbs," the press secretary said, extending her hand.

"Sure you are." Mrs. Tubbs kept her hands on her hips. Obviously, she was wondering how a gal was supposed to catch a man when there was always someone like "Donna" around to mess things up.

She turned her attention back to her new gentleman friend. "Vice-president?" she asked. "Vice-president of what?"

"Why, of the United States," Donna answered.

"You're the vice-pres. . . ?"

"That's right."

Donna took his arm. "If you'll excuse us," she said to Mrs. Tubbs, "I'd like to get some pictures of the vice-president talking to the vice-shah of Who-kares-ik-stan."

"Sure," Mrs. Tubbs smiled and stepped aside. "But don't keep him long. We must finish our conversation." As they walked away, she shouted after them, "When you come back, I'll give you my phone number. Then you can call me sometime."

Come back? Call Mrs. Tubbs? I don't think so. The poor man was practically running to get away from her.

"Ladies and gentlemen," a voice announced over the speaker. "The president of the United States—and the shah of Who-kares-ik-stan!"

The strains of "Hail to the Chief" filled the air as the president and the shah, along with their wives and half a dozen secret service men, strode out of the White House and into the Rose Garden.

The president and the shah waved and smiled to acknowledge the applause of the crowd. Then the president stepped behind the podium and signaled for silence.

"Mr. President!" a reporter shouted. "Is there any new information on those spies? Have we recovered that helicopter?"

The president shook his head. "I'll answer all of your questions later on. But right now, I want to introduce to you my very good friend—Abdul Gamal Zia Chou Nigurski Floddenhooper Jones—shah of the great country of Who-kares-ik-stan. We are very honored to have the shah here with us today, and we're delighted that he has brought us a wonderful, wonderful gift. Mr. Jones?" He motioned for the shah to step up to the microphone.

"Is my pleasure," he said, "to give to people of United States two of rarest animal in world. Only ten left."

He clapped his hands loudly, and two assistants came forward with a large box covered by a black tarp. They set it down where everyone could get a good view, then threw back the tarp.

"Our national rodent," the shah said. "Giant Who-kares-ik-stani rat!"

(He wasn't kidding when he said "giant." Those things were huge!)

"MEOWWWRRR!" Precious couldn't resist. He had never seen such fat, flavorful-looking rats! Immediately, he sprang toward their cage.

"Precious! Don't—" Mrs. Tubbs tried to hold on to his leash but let go after doing a nose-dive onto . . .

"OAFF!"

. . . the White House lawn. As she fell, her wig twisted around on her head so that her face was completely covered.

Meanwhile, the rat cage . . .

CRASH! BANGed!

Unfortunately, all the excitement was too much for Slobs to take sitting down. She'd had quite enough of this "good doggie" stuff, thank you. "RUFF! RUFF!"

Mrs. Tubbs scrambled to her feet and raced forward, trying to rescue her beloved cat. The only problem was that with the wig in her face, she couldn't see where she was going. "OUCH! OOOOOF!"

She ran smack-dab into the president, knocking him backward into the shah of Who-kares-ik-stan and . . .

KER-SPLASH!

. . . the three of them tumbled head-over-heels into the Rose Garden pond.

"Grab her!" shouted one of the secret service men.

Suddenly poor Mrs. Tubbs found herself in the grip of a half dozen more secret service guys. "You're under arrest!" one of them shouted.

"For what?" Mrs. Tubbs cried as she twisted her wig around to its proper position.

"For attacking the president of the United States!"

5

Monster on the Metro

MONDAY, 12:19 EDST

The rat cage bounced once . . .

BANG!

. . . twice . . .

CRASH!

. . . three times . . .

SMASH!

On the third bounce, its door flew open and the two rodents scurried out.

"Yowwrrrrrr!" Precious screeched to a stop.

Those rats were bigger than he thought. They were almost the size of sheep! And they weren't afraid of a house cat, either, even if he was three or four times fatter than an ordinary cat. They stood on their hind legs and slashed at the frightened cat with their long, sharp claws. So Precious fought back as best he could, by turning and running as fast as his legs could take him.

Meanwhile, Mrs. Tubbs was being marched off to jail. One tough secret agent had her left arm, one had her right arm, another stood behind her, and still another was in front of her. They weren't about to let her get away.

What the poor guys didn't know is that whenever she thinks Precious is in trouble, Mrs. Tubbs becomes a lean, mean fighting machine!

"Eee-yaw!"

WHACK!

A karate kick took care of the guy in front of her. "Yie-Heee-Uh!"

SMASH!

A jiujitsu smash to the stomach disabled the fellow behind her.

"NYUK! NYUK! NYUK!"
BOINK! BOINK!

And a good old-fashioned *Three Stooges* head-bang took care of the guys on either side of her.

"Nobody's going to hurt my kitty!" she yelled. Turning, she ran after him as fast as she could.

"Precious!" With every step she took, water from the pond squished out of her shoes. "Come to Mama! Come on, baby!"

But Precious wasn't listening! Up and down the Rose Garden he went, in and out among the bushes.

"Don't you . . . ow! . . . hurt my . . . ouch! . . . sweet . . . ow! ow! . . . little pussycat!" Mrs. Tubbs yelled at the rats as she ran through the rosebushes after him.

The secret service men, who had recovered from their blows, were right behind her.

"Come . . . ouch! . . . back here!" they yelled at Mrs. Tubbs. "You're . . . ow! ow! ow! . . . under arrest!"

(Somebody forgot to remind everyone that rosebushes have thorns!)

The chase finally led out of the White House Rose Garden, across Pennsylvania Avenue, and onto the Capitol Mall.

Fortunately for Sean and Melissa, Slobs was no longer in the race. Something else had captured her attention. She stopped, let the chase pass her, and began sniffing the ground. Suddenly she stiffened and stared at something in the distance.

"What is it, girl?" Melissa asked. "What do you see?"

Sean shaded his eyes with his right hand and looked. "I wish I knew what she was looking at," he said.

Even though Slobs, Sean, and Melissa were no longer in the chase, a hundred yards up the Capitol Mall, it continued.

Precious zigged, zagged, and then zigged again, trying to shake those stupid rats, but nothing seemed to work. Finally he zagged when he should have zigged! He didn't see the reflecting pool in front of the Lincoln Memorial until it was too late and . . .

KER-SPLASH! "MEOW!"

. . . into the water he went. Followed by the rats . . .

SPLASH! SPLASH!
"SQUEAK! SQUEAK!"

. . . who hated water even more than he did. And finally, Mrs. Tubbs . . .

KER-SPLAAASSSHHH!

. . . followed by the four secret service agents . . .
. . . fifteen newspaper reporters . . .
. . . thirteen television photographers, and, finally . . .

. . . twenty-seven tourists, who decided to jump into the water just because everyone else was doing it!

Despite all the splashing and shouting, Slobs never moved. Her tail stood straight up, her eyes stared straight ahead.

Suddenly Sean shouted, "I see him!"

"See who?" Melissa cried. She turned to see her brother wearing his X-ray glasses again.

"Someone's hiding behind that tree over there!"

"Where?" Melissa asked. "I don't see anybody."

"There!" Sean shouted. "He's spying on us!"

Slobs whined and began sniffing at the air. She drooled as if she smelled something good to eat.

Sean pointed toward the tree. "Hey, you!" he yelled. "Why are you watching us?" Then, turning to Slobs, he shouted, "Sic him, girl!"

"GRRRRRRR! WOOF! WOOF!"

Slobs was off like a rocket. Although she was really a big softy who had never hurt anyone or anything, her bark sounded fierce.

"Yikes!" The spy dropped his binoculars and took off, sprinting toward the nearest subway entrance.

"It's the mustache man from the hotel," Sean shouted.

"You're right!" Melissa exclaimed.

The spy managed to reach the subway entrance just ahead of Slobs. He scrambled down the escalator and disappeared into the crowd waiting for the next train.

The huge dog stood at the top of the escalator, barking and yapping.

"We'll never find him on the Metro," Sean groaned.

"Slobs can find him!" Melissa insisted.

"In this crowd?" Sean asked. "I don't think so."

Hundreds of people made their way up and down the escalators, into and out of the Metro station.

"Come on," Melissa said. "We've got to try."

"You're right," Sean said. He bent down and fastened Slobs' leash. "Let's go, girl," he said, patting her on the head.

"WOAF!" Slobs answered.

Sean bought tickets from the nearest machine, and the three of them scampered down the escalator onto the platform.

"Hey, duds, what's down?" someone said.

Sean looked at his digital wristwatch. Sure enough, Jeremiah's glowing green face smiled up at him.

"Jeremiah!" Sean whispered. "Listen, I don't want to hurt your feelings, but we're doing something really important right now. Could you possibly come back later?"

"K.O.," Jeremiah replied. "I'll just go somewhere else. See you later, crocodile."

"Alligator," Melissa said. "It's 'See you later, alligator.' "

But Jeremiah wasn't listening. His face had already disappeared from Sean's watch . . . then reappeared on the monitors announcing departure and arrival times for subway trains.

"How's this, duds?" his voice echoed throughout the terminal. Dozens of monitors lined the walls of the station, and Jeremiah's face stared out from every one of them. "Hello, folks," he called out.

Jeremiah meant well. He was just trying to be friendly. But it didn't work. There's only one way to describe what happened over the next three minutes: TOTAL PANIC!

"Aaaggghhh!" a woman screamed as she pointed at Jeremiah. "A monster!"

"A monster?" Jeremiah cried. "Where? Where's a monster?!" He began shaking with fear. "Well, you know what they say. He who hesitates is monster food. I'm out of here."

With that, Jeremiah was gone, but it didn't stop the panic.

Sean and Melissa stood with their backs pressed against the wall as hundreds of people ran past them. And soon, believe it or not, the entire station was empty.

Well, not exactly.

Because over in the corner a man stood all by himself. And he seemed to be talking into his necktie! He had pulled the bottom of the tie up to his mouth and was definitely having a conversation with it.

Suddenly there was a chirping noise from somewhere on his body. "Pardon me," he said to his tie. "My socks are ringing."

"It's him," Melissa whispered. "It's the mustache man!"

He yanked off a shoe, pulled his foot up toward his mouth, and began talking. "Double Oh Zero here," he said. "I'm afraid you've called the wrong number. No, this is not Paul's Pizza Parlor. Yes, I'm certain. I'm sure you are hungry, sir, but I'm—" Suddenly he noticed Sean and Melissa watching him. "Outta here!"

The young detectives were about to close in when suddenly . . .

SHHHHHH . . . EEEEE!

. . . a train pulled into the station.

Doors opened, turnstiles whirled, as a hundred

more people spilled through them. And somehow, some way, the mystery man melted into the crowd.

"Where'd he go?" Sean shouted.

"I don't know!" Melissa answered. "He was right in front of us and then . . . There he is!" She pointed at one of the subway cars.

Sure enough, the "spy guy" was standing in the car, hanging on to an overhead strap, and smiling at them through the window as if to say, "Beat ya!"

"Let's go!" Melissa exclaimed. "The train's about to leave!" She sprinted for the train and barely made it through the door before it closed.

Slobs made it, too.

Sean wasn't so fortunate. He was just starting through the door when it slammed shut on him. Normally, a door on a subway train will bounce back open if it hits someone. But not this one. Apparently, it was broken.

"Sean!" Melissa screamed. "Are you okay?"

"I'm stuck!" he cried. "You've gotta help me!"

Melissa grabbed hold of his hand and pulled.

"It's no use. I can't budge you!"

Shhhh . . .

Thunk . . . Thunk . . . Thunk . . .

The train shuddered and slowly pulled away from the platform.

69

"Come on, sis! Pull!"

"I am pulling!"

THUNK THUNK THUNK . . .

The train moved faster!

"WOOF! WOOF! WOOF!" Slobs ran around in circles and barked, but nobody moved from their seats to give Sean and Melissa a hand.

"Misty!" Sean shouted. "I'm falling!"

She could feel him slipping away.

"Uhhhhhhhh!" Her muscles strained as she pulled on her brother's arms with every bit of her strength. If Sean fell, he would be run over and killed. She didn't say anything, but her mind was screaming, *God, help me! Please!*

"Pull harder!" he shouted.

"It's no use," she cried. "I can't do it!"

Tears streamed down her cheeks as she looked into her brother's panic-stricken face. What would life be like without him?!

6

Sean and Melissa's Wild Ride

MONDAY, 14:08 EDST

Sean looked down at the subway tracks speeding beneath him. Without a miracle, death was only seconds away. He looked up into the subway car.

Melissa's face was pressed against the glass as she tried desperately to hold on to his arms. Those arms were the only part of his body safely inside the car. She pulled as hard as she could, but her strength was almost spent.

"Melissa!" he shouted. "One more time! Give it all you've got!"

Her face reddened as she pulled, giving him one final, desperate yank until . . .

SHHHHHHH!

. . . the door suddenly swished open! As Melissa

yanked, Sean flew into the car and . . .

KER-THUNK!

. . . landed hard on his stomach, safely inside the car.

Immediately, Slobs was on top of him, covering his face with doggie kisses.

"What happened?" he asked when he finally caught his breath. "How did you get the door open?"

"I don't know." Melissa was crying and laughing at the same time. "I prayed," she said. "And I guess God just gave us a miracle!"

"I guess He did," Sean said. "I guess He did!"

MONDAY, 14:27 EDST

By the time the subway reached the D-Street station, Sean had almost stopped shaking.

"This is our stop," Melissa said. "Looks like it's his stop, too!"

"His?" Sean asked. "Who?" And then he saw him. "Oh yeah."

Mustache Man . . . Sock Phone Man . . . Agent Double Oh Zero . . . whatever you want to call him didn't see them as he quickly left the train. Pushing past others, Sean and Melissa managed to get out of the train and follow. They were about twenty yards behind him as he walked briskly up the street, his head down, his eyes focused on the sidewalk.

"Where's he going?" Melissa asked.

"I think I know," Sean answered.

"You do?" Melissa asked.

"I'm sure he's one of those spies we keep hearing about," he answered. "If we follow him, I'll bet we'll find out where the rest of them are hiding."

"Not unless they're hiding in our hotel," Melissa said.

"What?"

"Look," Melissa pointed.

Sure enough, ol' what's his name had entered their hotel by a side door. The young detectives followed close behind.

THUMP! THUMP! THUMP!

His footsteps echoed in the stairwell as he raced up the stairs to the second floor. Bloodhounds, Inc., stayed hot on his trail.

THUMP! THUMP! THUMP!

Third floor.

THUMP! THUMP! THUMP!

Fourth floor. Sean, Melissa, and Slobs paused a

moment to catch their breath and waited for the footsteps to continue.

And waited . . .

And waited some more . . .

But all they heard was silence.

"What's he doing?" Melissa whispered.

"Maybe he knows we're following him," Sean suggested.

"What if he's hiding up there, waiting to attack us?" Melissa asked.

Sean shrugged. "I guess that's a chance we'll have to take." He gestured politely up the stairs. "Ladies first."

"Oh no," Melissa shook her head. "Age before beauty."

"I insist."

"No! I insist!"

They might have gone on like that for hours—or days—if Melissa had not come up with a brilliant idea.

"Let's go together," she said.

"Agreed," Sean nodded.

Moving as quietly as possible, they tiptoed up the stairs, stopping at the door that led out to the fourth floor. Carefully they peeked around the corner and saw that . . .

Nobody was there.

Sean ran on up to the fifth floor, then quickly came back down.

"Any sign of him?" Melissa asked.

"Nothing." He shook his head. "I don't get it! Where could he have gone? I never heard a door open, did you?"

Melissa shook her head. "It's like he disappeared. *Poof!* Just like that!"

"Yeah, like a ghost!" Sean agreed.

Melissa snapped her fingers. "I've got an idea! Have you got your X-ray glasses?"

Sean patted his pants pocket with a grin. "Right here."

"Well?" she asked.

"Well, what?"

"Well, maybe he's hiding somewhere. If so, you'll be able to see him with those glasses."

"Good idea! Glad I thought of it," Sean said. He pulled the glasses out of his pocket and quickly put them on. He looked up. He looked down. He turned in a complete circle. Then he shook his head. "I don't see anything unusual," he sighed. "Just wood and steel and . . ."

He knocked on the wall with his hand and . . . suddenly the floor disappeared!

Sean, Melissa, and Slobs began falling . . . down,

down, down! Moving faster and faster!

"EEEAAAGGHH!" Sean and Melissa screamed as their hair stood straight up.

"AROOOOOO!" Slobs howled as her ears stood straight up.

MONDAY, 12:02 PDST

Meanwhile, back at Doc's house, the gardener she had just hired stood in her doorway with his hat in his hands.

"I'm sorry, lady," he said, "but this is going to cost you a lot more than I thought."

She frowned and shook her head. She had hired him to trim a few bushes around the sides of her house. She didn't understand why she should have to pay any more than the price they had settled on.

The gardener fidgeted nervously with his hat. "It's just that . . . as soon as we cut those plants, they grow back."

Doc looked puzzled, and the gardener kept talking.

"And, ma'am, I understood that you had a few bushes that needed to be cut back." He shook his head. "I don't know what your definition of 'few' is, but you've got a jungle out there."

Doc produced a pad and pencil and wrote, *What are you talking about?*

"Follow me," the man said, "and I'll show you."

With Doc right behind him, the man strode out to the side of the house where he and his partner had been working.

And he was right . . . it *was* a jungle.

Azalea bushes that had been eighteen inches high just a few days ago now towered over Doc's head. Sunflowers stood nearly as tall as the nearby streetlights. And daffodils were big enough to sit on. Everywhere you looked, there were plants, plants, and more plants. And vines. They snaked their way up the side of her house and onto the roof. They both watched as the gardener's partner, dripping with perspiration, attacked one of them with a power saw.

He finished cutting all the way through, stepped back, and . . .

SHHOOOOOP!

. . . in less than five seconds, a new vine grew back to take its place.

"See, lady," the gardener said. "Like I said, as soon as we cut them, they grow back. So we're going to have to charge you a little bit more."

77

Doc didn't answer.

"Lady?" He turned around to find out why she wasn't answering. Doc had dashed off, nowhere to be found.

7

Hildagard Tubbs: Terrorist?!

MONDAY, 15:07 EDST

For a moment, Sean thought he was dead.

Then he realized he was sitting on the floor in a place that looked very much like the control room at Dad's radio station. The walls were crowded with electronic equipment. All around him, hundreds of tiny lights blinked on and off. On one wall, a bank of TV monitors showed pictures from various points throughout the city.

As his eyes grew accustomed to the dim light, Sean saw Melissa sitting beside him. "Are you okay?" he asked.

"I'm fine," she answered.

"Where's Slobs?"

"Over there." Melissa pointed across the room,

where the big dog was already investigating things by running around and sniffing like crazy.

"What happened?" Sean asked.

"I guess you hit the right spot on the wall," Melissa said.

"I know that," Sean answered. "But what I mean is, we fell so far, how come we're not . . ."

"Dead?" Melissa finished his question.

"Yeah, dead," Sean replied.

"I can answer that question," someone said.

"Who's there?" Sean and Melissa asked at the same time.

"I am."

Suddenly they saw the man they had been following standing and looking down at them.

"You weren't really falling," he said. "You were traveling in a sub-supersonic arc of—no, wait a minute. You were traveling in a supersubsonic spiral. No, that ain't it. Shucks, guess I can't explain it after all. Anyway, I've been waiting for you." He held out his hand to help Melissa to her feet.

"You have?" Melissa asked, taking his hand.

"Yup. Oh, I almost forgot. 'A wet bird never flies backward,' " he said.

"Huh?" Sean asked as he stood and began slapping the dust off of his pants.

" 'A wet bird never flies backward,' " he repeated.

Sean frowned, then exchanged looks with Melissa.

The man looked confused. "Aren't you, uh, 49 and 78?" he asked.

"No, sir," Melissa answered. "I'm thirteen and Sean'll be fifteen next month."

"I mean," the man asked, "you're not secret agents 49 and 78?"

"No, sir," Sean replied, "we're Bloodhounds, Incorporated."

"Really?" the man asked. "Well, I'm Agent Double Oh Zero—United States Secret Service."

"Wow!" Sean exclaimed.

The man smiled. "My friends call me Trip . . . short for Triple Zero. Anyway, I was watching you at the White House because I was supposed to make contact with two new secret agents there. And you kind of fit their description."

"We do?" Melissa asked.

"Sort of," Trip said. "Except you're awfully young."

Sean shook his head. "I don't understand. If you thought we were secret agents, why did you run from us?"

"I didn't run from you!" Trip sounded indignant. "If I hadn't wanted you to see me, you never would have seen me. I led you back here. With this."

He reached beneath his shirt and pulled out a pork chop.

Slobs came running.

"I knew that dog of yours could smell this from a mile away," he said as he tossed her the chop. Slobs grabbed it and ran into the corner to devour it. Then the secret agent dug into his pocket and pulled out a small photograph. "By the way," he said to Sean, "here's a great picture of you stuck in the subway door."

"You saw that?" Sean asked. "Then why didn't you try to help me?"

"Try?" the man said. "Who do you think opened the door for you?"

"You?" Sean asked.

The secret agent pulled a ball-point pen out of his shirt pocket. "I did it with this," he said. "You see, all I have to do is press this clicker and . . ." Suddenly a stream of thick blue ink shot from the pen all over his face.

"Pttt . . . pttt . . . pttt . . ." he sputtered. He grabbed a handkerchief out of his pocket and dabbed the ink from his face. "Well, maybe it wasn't that clicker," he said. "Maybe it was this one." He pulled a tiny microcassette tape recorder out of his pants pocket and pressed the Play button.

WHOOOOSHHhhh . . .

Flames shot out from the back of Trip's shoes, propelling him across the room and . . .

KA-POW!

. . . face-first into the wall.

"Oww . . ." he groaned as he slid down the wall and crumpled onto the floor. "I hate it when that happens." A blue circle of ink was left on the wall where his nose had smashed into it.

Pulling himself together, he rose and staggered back across the room. "I guess that button starts the little rocket engines in my shoes," he grinned. "So I guess it must be this—"

"We believe you!" Sean cried.

"Just don't push any more buttons!" Melissa yelled.

Trip shrugged. "Okee-dokee. By the way," he motioned to Sean, "you've got something in your hair."

Sean rubbed at his hair, and a small flower fell onto the floor.

"Hmm?" Sean said. "Must be a blossom from a cherry tree. Washington is full of them."

Melissa looked at him, not so sure. This was the third or fourth time vegetation had appeared in her brother's hair. What was going on?

MONDAY, 12:19 PDST

Back at Doc's house, the gardener found her in her den, typing away at her computer keyboard.

"Excuse me, ma'am," he said.

Because her back was to him, she didn't know he was there and didn't answer.

"Ma'am . . ."

He moved closer to tap her on the shoulder. But before he did, he decided to sneak a peek at what she was typing:

FROM: nius.com
To: Bloodhounds, Inc.
Subject: X-ray glasses
Priority: Urgent

Sean, Melissa, do not use the X-ray glasses I gave you. Have discovered the subatomic beta frequency is very dangerous when combined with the bleems. Repeated use has adverse effect on plant life. Plants grow like crazy. Don't know if there are other problems. Let me know that you got this message. Doc

Meanwhile, back in the . . . er, wherever Sean and Melissa were, Agent Double Oh Zero—or Trip, as his friends called him—walked over to a desk, opened a drawer, and pulled out a small silver gun.

"He's got a gun!" Melissa shouted.

Trip spun around. "Who's got a gun?"

"You do!" Melissa shouted, pointing at the pistol in his hand.

Trip looked down at the firearm in his hand and chuckled. "This isn't a gun. It's a remote-control device. I was just going to change the channel on one of these monitors so I can see what's going on at the White House. Watch!"

He pointed the device at one of the monitors and pulled the trigger.

KA-BLAM! CRASH!
KA-BLOOEY!

The monitor exploded as a bullet ripped into it.

"Well, what do you know," Trip said. "I guess this is a gun after all." He put it back in the drawer, rummaged around, and pulled out an ordinary-looking remote control. "I guess this must be the remote control," he said. "Funny how I get those two mixed up."

"Trip," Sean asked, "are you sure you work for the government?"

"Absolutely," the secret agent replied. "Hah! Just because I haven't solved a case in eighteen years, people think I'm washed-up. But I've had a run of bad luck, that's all. Say, have you seen my remote control?"

"You're holding it," Sean replied.

"Holding what?" Trip asked.

"Never mind," Sean sighed. "Listen, we have a detective agency back home in Midvale, and we'd love to help you, if that's okay."

"Yeah!" Melissa chimed in. "I don't mean to brag, but we're pretty good."

"Really!" Trip said. "I'd love to have your help! I'll swear you in as junior agents."

He looked up at the bank of TV monitors where one was still smoking. "These spies are really clever," he said. "Besides, with all these Civil War ghosts running around getting in the way . . . Look! There's one now!"

Sure enough, one of the monitors revealed a ghostly figure moving down one of the hotel's halls.

"But there's no such things as ghosts," Melissa argued.

"There isn't? How can you be so sure?"

"We've always found there's a rational explanation to what's happening," Sean said.

Melissa agreed. "Besides, the Bible says when we

die we go to face God. We don't hang around and
haunt hotels."

"I wouldn't be so sure," Trip said, staring back at
the monitor.

Melissa moved in for a better look. "Hmm. Did
they have digital watches during the Civil War?" she
asked.

"Of course not," Trip answered. "Why?"

"Because that 'ghost' is wearing one." She turned to
Trip. "Have you ever suspected that these ghosts might
have something to do with the spies you're looking
for?"

"Well, I uh . . ."

BRRRR . . . BRRRR

Before he could answer, a phone began ringing
somewhere nearby.

Trip lifted his necktie up to his mouth. "Hello," he
said. But the phone kept ringing.

Next, he tried a cuff link. "Hello?" No luck.

Next, he answered his wallet. "Hello?" Nope.

His belt . . . Nope. His eyeglasses . . . Nope.

And still the phone kept ringing.

Finally, he grinned. "Of course, it's my socks." He
pulled off his shoe, raised his foot, and spoke into it.

Sean and Melissa traded looks as he spoke.

"What's that?" Trip said. "At the Washington Monument? Yes, sir, I'm right on it." Lowering his foot, he turned to the kids and shouted, "There's trouble at the Lincoln Memorial!"

"Washington Monument!" Melissa corrected him.

"Yeah, like I said!" He slipped on his shoe and hurried to a nearby monitor. He clicked a button, and the Washington Monument appeared on a screen. At the moment, some lunatic was hanging out of a window near the top of the monument, waving her arms and screaming. Some lunatic that looked an awful lot like . . .

"Mrs. Tubbs!" Melissa gasped.

"You're right!" Sean cried. "It is Mrs. Tubbs!"

"Yes, I recognize that woman," Trip said. "She's the one who tried to beat up the president. And now she's . . . she's . . . er, well, whatever she's up to, we've got to stop her!"

8

Mrs. Tubbs Falls From Power

The monitor showed that a large crowd was gathering at the base of the Washington Monument. And for good reason. Mrs. Tubbs was dangling from a window more than five hundred feet above the ground!

Folks seemed to think she was a daredevil trapeze artist and this was all part of her act.

"Aeeee!" she screamed as she slipped another couple of inches.

"Hurrah!" the crowd screamed below.

"Peanuts! Get your peanuts!" a vendor shouted, pushing his cart.

"They think it's a party!" Sean exclaimed.

"We've got to do something!" Melissa yelled.

"Follow me!" Trip said. "We can be there in five minutes!"

Mrs. Tubbs slipped another couple of inches.

"I'm not sure we've got five minutes!" Melissa cried.

MONDAY, 16:11 EDST

It took four minutes and twenty-nine seconds to reach the Washington Monument.

Although she'd slipped a couple more inches, Mrs. Tubbs was still dangling from the window when they got there. Beneath her, people had spread blankets on the ground and were enjoying hot dogs and sodas. Some were taking part in a rousing sing-along.

Everyone was having fun.

Everyone except Mrs. Tubbs.

"Help me!" she screamed. "Somebody help me!"

A siren sounded off in the distance.

"Maybe they're bringing a hook and ladder," Melissa said hopefully.

Sean shook his head. "Even if they do, there's no ladder that high."

"He's right," Trip said. "We'll have to go up and get her ourselves!"

So, with Trip leading the way, Sean, Melissa, and Slobs ran into the monument and raced up the stairs.

It seemed pretty obvious that Double Oh Zero wasn't the brightest candle on the cake. But he was strong. And fast! He bounded up the stairs, taking two or three at a time.

Sean and Melissa had to stop for a rest every fifty steps or so, but Trip kept on going, with Slobs right on his heels. The kids were about two-thirds of the way to the top when they heard Trip shout, "Don't worry, Mrs. Tibbs, I've got you!"

Then they heard something else . . .

THUNK! CLUNK! BUMBLE!

. . . followed by his voice yelling, "Help! Somebody help me! Help me!"

The young detectives looked at each other.

"Oh no!" Sean said.

"He couldn't have," Melissa groaned.

"Come on, let's go!" Sean shouted.

They raced up the stairs as fast as they could.

When they got to the top, Trip was nowhere to be seen. Slobs had a firm grip on Mrs. Tubbs' sweater and was attempting to pull the woman to safety. But the dog whined and growled as her toenails slipped and skidded on the floor.

Sean and Melissa ran to the edge of window and looked over to see . . .

Sure enough, Trip was dangling below Mrs. Tubbs, who was hanging upside down with her sweater caught on the ledge. The only thing that kept Trip from falling was her grip on his suspenders.

"Good catch," Sean said to Mrs. Tubbs.

"Why, thank you," she gasped.

From down below, Trip looked up to them and sheepishly called, "I guess I slipped."

"It's okay," Sean said. "We'll save you."

He and Melissa each grabbed hold of one of Mrs. Tubbs' legs and began to pull. Slowly . . . very slowly . . . inch by inch . . . Mrs. Tubbs . . . and Trip . . . were dragged back inside to safety.

Down below, the crowd erupted into cheers and applause.

After waving to the crowd, Mrs. Tubbs turned to the kids. "Thank you!" she panted. "Thank you! You saved my life!"

"Mine too!" Trip said.

As soon as Melissa caught her breath, she asked Mrs. Tubbs, "What happened? How did you manage to fall out the window?"

"I was trying to rescue my cat."

"Precious? In here? But how?" Sean asked.

"Those horrible rats chased him in here," she said. "Poor thing."

"And by the way," Melissa asked, "how did you get out of jail?"

"They had the whole thing on videotape," Mrs. Tubbs explained. "When they looked at it, they knew I wasn't trying to hurt President Shrub, so they let me go."

"And then?"

"Precious and I went back to the White House to apologize to the president. Well, when those horrible animals that had been hiding saw Precious, they just went crazy and . . ."

"Where's Precious now?" Sean asked.

"I don't know." She pointed at a worn spot on the floor. "I slipped right there," she said. "If my sweater hadn't caught on the ledge . . ." Her voice trailed off.

Suddenly for the first time she really noticed Trip. She reached up and patted her hair into place. "I don't believe we've been formally introduced."

An hour and a half later, Slobs finally found Precious—sound asleep in President Lincoln's lap at the Lincoln Memorial.

The rats, however, were still at large. (In fact, the next time you're in Washington, keep an eye open for them. And make sure you don't bring your cat!)

MONDAY, 18:00 SHARP PDST

Back in Midvale, Frieda Smedlap slowly shuffled out of her house to pick up the afternoon newspaper. Her slippers made a soft . . .

*SFFFT . . . SFFFT . . . SFFFT*ing

. . . sound as they padded against the driveway.

By the way, Mrs. Smedlap was vice-president of the Garden Club, and she had never liked Mrs. Tubbs. When she bent over to pick up the paper, she froze in disbelief. Because there, staring back at her, was a huge photograph of Hildagard Tubbs hanging out of the Washington Monument.

The headline above the photograph read:

**"Garden Club President Runs Amok
in Nation's Capital."**

For a moment, Mrs. Smedlap thought she was going to faint. *How could that woman embarrass us like this?* she thought.

Then another thought came that made her smile. . . . *Why, I do believe the Garden Club is going to need a new president. I'd better start writing my acceptance speech.*

9

Sean Hunter:
Flower Child

TUESDAY, 8:24 EDST

When Sean and Melissa reached the command center the next morning, Trip was already there, keeping a close watch on his large bank of TV monitors.

"The spies have struck again," he said.

"Where?" Sean asked.

"They stole the plans to the government's new anti-anti-anti-missile-missile-missile system," he said. "Sneaked into the Pentagon and grabbed them yesterday afternoon while everyone was watching all the excitement at the Washington Monument."

"And they're no closer to finding that helicopter?" Sean asked.

"That's right."

Sean ran his hand through his hair, and three or four cherry blossoms fell out. "How weird," he said. "I wonder why that keeps happening."

Melissa didn't answer. Her attention was on monitor number 6.

"Look!" she exclaimed. "Isn't that the ghost we were following the other night?"

The monitor showed a close-up of a young businessman dressed in a dark suit and tie.

"Ghost?" Sean asked. "Melissa, that guy doesn't look anything like—"

"Look closer!" she insisted.

Trip hit a button, bringing the man into a close-up on the monitor.

"Look at his nose," Melissa said.

Sean nodded. "Yes, his nose is bent a little bit, like that ghost, but that still doesn't—"

"And the eyebrows. Look at the eyebrows."

"Hmm." Sean was beginning to see what Melissa was talking about. The man's eyebrows were especially thick, and they ran in one continuous line.

"That's him," Melissa insisted. "I know it is!" She pointed at the monitor. "Where is this coming from?"

"The hotel lobby," Trip said.

"Let's follow this guy and find out what he's up to," Melissa said.

"Agreed," Sean nodded.

He pulled his X-ray glasses out of his shirt pocket. "I'll wear these to make sure we don't lose him."

"Oh, Sean," Melissa complained. "Do you always have to wear those?"

"Come on!" he said, ignoring her. "Let's go!"

TUESDAY, 15:07 EDST

"Well, if he's a ghost, he's a pretty boring one," Sean said. "We've been following him all day, and he hasn't done anything exciting."

"So why don't you take those glasses off," Melissa said. "You must be getting a headache."

At that moment, a woman passing by smiled at Sean, held up two fingers, and said, "Peace, brother."

"What did she say that for?" Sean asked.

"She was just being friendly, I guess."

"Far out!" someone else said.

"Groovy, man, groovy!" another laughed.

"What's going on?" Sean asked.

Melissa gasped. "You've got flowers in your hair."

"Again? Well, brush them out, will you?"

"No, not like that! *Big* flowers!"

"Then pull them out!"

Melissa grabbed a couple of the daisies in her brother's hair and yanked.

"Ow!" Sean exclaimed. "That hurt!"

"But I got them," Melissa said. "See?"

She handed them to her brother.

"Uuuhhh!" she inhaled sharply.

"What?" Sean asked. "What happened?"

"They just grew back," Melissa said.

"Why do these things always happen to me?" Sean moaned. "And besides, I think I'm—AH-AH-AH-allergic! CHOOOOO!"

"We'll have to get you some allergy medicine," Melissa said. "But first, I think you need a hat." She looked around and saw a sports shop across the street. "Maybe we can find something in there," she said.

"What do you think?" Melissa asked.

Sean had lifted up his glasses to study himself in the mirror. A Washington Redskins cap covered his hair and the flowers in it.

"Pretty good," he said. "And if the flowers are covered, I don't think they're going to bother me so much."

"Hellooo! Is anybody home?" The voice came from Sean's digital watch.

Sean looked down and spotted their little buddy. "Jeremiah! What's up?"

"You have an f-mail from Doc," he answered.

"F-mail?" Melissa asked. "You mean 'e-mail'?"

"Whatever. She sent it yesterday."

"Yesterday?" Melissa asked. "Why didn't we get it then?"

Jeremiah's face turned from glowing green to glowing red. "I'm afraid I was on the outernet."

"Internet," Sean corrected.

"Anyway, I had your line chained down."

"Tied up?" Melissa asked.

"Yeah, that," Jeremiah shrugged. "Anyway, I was studying some history. Did you know that in ancient Egypt, everyone wrote in hydraulics?"

"Hieroglyph—" Melissa started to correct him.

But Sean interrupted. "What about that e-mail?"

"Coming right down!" Jeremiah said.

He disappeared, and the e-mail popped up on the screen.

Sean began reading. "So that's it!" he suddenly shouted. "It's the X-ray glasses!"

Melissa grabbed his arm so she could read Doc's message for herself. "That's why my petunias grew so big back home!" she exclaimed.

"And that's why I've got all these flowers in my hair," Sean groaned.

"Don't worry," Melissa said. "If you stop wearing the glasses, the flowers will die . . . eventually." Suddenly she put her hand over her mouth to stifle a giggle. "I just thought of something," she laughed.

"What's that?" Sean asked.

"That guy we've been following and who you've been looking at all these hours, he's bound to wake up in the morning . . ."

" . . . with flowers in his hair, too!" Sean laughed.

Melissa continued to giggle. "Well, it's good to know you're not alone in this!"

TUESDAY, 15:42 EDST

BRRRR! BRRRR!

"Bloodhounds, Incorporated," Sean said as he answered his cell phone. "Oh, hi, Trip. What's up?"

Trip answered, "I just got a call from General Accounting. There's been another break-in. And . . ."

"Yes?"

"Whoever it was left flowers all over the place."

"Flowers?" Sean asked.

"Yeah," Trip said, "flowers. Can you come over here and keep an eye on things while I check it out?"

"We'll be right there!" Sean said.

TUESDAY, 16:07 EDST

When they arrived, Trip was pacing back and forth, wearing another one of his "spectacular" disguises. This one included a beard and a black top hat. (Melissa didn't want to say anything, but she thought he looked an awful lot like Abraham Lincoln.)

"Thanks for coming so fast," Trip said. "Just keep an eye on these monitors, and . . . oh, I almost forgot." He reached into his jacket pocket and pulled out what appeared to be a tiny garage-door opener. "If either one of you gets in trouble, push this button. It will let me know exactly where you are, and I'll come right away."

Sean and Melissa exchanged meaningful glances.

"I know what you're thinking," Trip said. "But I guarantee you. This will work."

TUESDAY, 18:14 EDST

Nearly two hours passed, and Sean was getting frustrated. "We should be doing something," he complained.

"Like what?" Melissa asked.

"I don't know. Anything!"

"Look!" Melissa pointed at one of the monitors.

The ghostly looking soldier strode past. He didn't realize that a garden of flowers was growing in his hair, leaving a trail of petals behind him as he "drifted" down the hall.

"Let's go!" Sean cried.

"Where?"

"After him!" Sean exclaimed. "He's leaving the perfect trail."

"Maybe we ought to wait until Trip gets back," Melissa said.

"No way!" Sean argued. "We'll follow the trail of flower petals, find out what room he's in, and lead the authorities right to him."

"I don't know . . ." Melissa hesitated.

But if there was one thing Sean was good at, it was nagging. And, like it or not, ten minutes later, they were back in the hotel hallway. Slobs led the way as Sean and Melissa followed the flower petals all the way to the door of . . . room 570.

"I knew it!" Sean whispered. "I told you something was going on in there!"

"Listen," Melissa whispered.

They leaned toward the door and heard all sorts of moaning, groaning, and ghostly noises floating from the room.

Once again, Sean pulled his X-ray glasses out of his pocket.

"Sean, do you really think you should be doing that?" Melissa asked.

"One last time," he promised as he slipped them on. "After that I'll . . . woah!"

"What do you see?" Melissa asked.

"Nothing," he frowned. "It's empty. Just like before."

He took out his Swiss Army knife.

"You're not going to pick the lock, are you?" asked Melissa. "You could get us in a lot of trouble."

Sean sighed. "I'm doing it for our country, Misty."

Melissa glanced about nervously as he continued to work.

"These old locks ought to be easy to—"

CLICK!

"There!" he said as he pushed open the door.

Cautiously, the young detectives tiptoed into the room.

It was empty, just as Sean said. Except for one thing . . . A tiny speaker sat on the table. A tiny speaker that was giving off all the ghostly noises.

"What's that about?" Sean asked.

Melissa shook her head as she reached over and picked it up. "I don't know, but here's our ghost."

Meanwhile, Slobs was whining and scratching at the closet door.

"What is it, girl?" Sean whispered. He crept toward the door. Once he arrived, he carefully grabbed the doorknob and yanked it open to reveal . . .

Nothing.

"It's just a closet," Sean complained.

"GRRRR! GRRRR!"

"Slobs doesn't think so," Melissa said.

Sean nodded and stepped inside to investigate. He pushed against the back wall, trying to find something, anything that was unusual. But once again, he came up empty.

"Maybe if we turned the light on, we could get a better look. Here," Melissa said as she flipped the switch to turn on the closet light.

But it wasn't the closet light!

Instead, the back wall of the closet suddenly slid

up. Before them stood a dark, narrow stairway that led straight up.

"Well, will you look at that," Sean said.

"Where does it go?" Melissa asked.

"There's only one way to find out."

As if agreeing, Slobs let out a bark and ran up the stairs until she completely disappeared.

"Well," Sean said nervously, "what are we waiting for?"

Melissa swallowed. "I can think of a few things."

"Come on," he said. "Let's go!"

10

Your Average Garden-Variety Spies

TUESDAY, 18:32 EDST

There was light up above. Sean and Melissa could hear voices. They climbed higher and higher until they realized they were approaching the roof. They arrived and carefully stepped up from the stairway and onto the tar and gravel surface.

The voices were much louder.

They tiptoed around the corner and saw not one, not two, but three men in Civil War uniforms. They stood in front of a large machine that was covered with a tarp.

"I bet that's the *Dragonfly*," Sean whispered.

"The what?" Melissa asked.

"That helicopter the spies stole."

"You mean—"

"Shh . . ." Sean whispered. "Listen."

"So then it is agreed," the oldest of the three men said. He appeared to be the leader. "We will leave the country tonight."

"Yes, Gregor!" the man next to him said. "With many secrets to help our homeland bring these American dogs to their knees!"

"It was a brilliant idea, Sergei, to use that old legend about ghosts as our cover," Gregor said. "Again, we will meet here on the hotel roof in four hours' time. Then we will fly away."

"GRRRRR! GRRRRR!"

Melissa grabbed Slobs and tried to quiet her.

Gregor laughed and poked Sergei in the stomach. "My dear friend, I hear your stomach growling. You have been eating too much American food."

"It was not my stomach," Sergei protested.

Gregor turned to the other man and asked, "Was it yours?"

The other man shook his head.

"We'd better get out of here," Sean whispered. He turned to go.

They headed back to the stairway and almost made it through the doorway, except for the part of Sean bumping into it. No problem, except for the part where it knocked off his Washington Redskins cap and allowed all those wonderful petals in his hair to fall into his face. Even that wouldn't have been a problem, except for his allergies.

"AH . . . AH . . . AH . . ."

He did his best to fight it, but . . .

" . . . CHOOOOOO!"

. . . his best wasn't good enough.

"Someone's at the stairs!" Gregor shouted. "Get them!"

"Run!" Sean shouted. "Run!"

Good idea. Unfortunately, Sean's version of running involved tripping over his Redskins cap and crashing into Melissa. Again, no problem, except for the part where they both wound up in a tangle on the stairway.

And before they could get to their feet . . . the spies had them!

Sean shoved his hand into his pants pocket and frantically fumbled. Where was that emergency thing with the button Trip had given him?

Gregor's strong hands closed on his shoulders and lifted him to his feet. "My boy," he said. "You are in very much trouble."

Ah . . . there it was! Now, if he could just get his finger on the button . . .

When Trip came out of the Congressional Office Building, he was shocked to find Mrs. Tubbs waiting near his car.

"Oooo, I like your costume," she cooed, referring to his Abraham Lincoln disguise. "You look so . . . presidential!"

"Mrs. Tibbs," he said. "What are you doing here?"

"Tubbs," she corrected him. "I just happened to be in the neighborhood and—"

"You just happened to—"

"Okay, I followed you," she confessed. "Is that so bad? I just thought maybe we could have a nice dinner together, and perhaps take in a movie, or . . ."

EEEEEEE!

She stopped in mid-sentence. "What is that horrible sound!"

Trip reached into his jacket pocket and pulled out something that looked like a handheld calculator. Whatever it was, it was giving off a high-pitched, screeching sound.

"It's them!" he said.

"Them, who?"

"We've got to go, Mrs. Tipps. They're on the roof!"

"It's Tubbs!" she said. "And what roof?"

"I'll explain on the way! But we don't have time to drive. We'll have to fly!"

"Fly?" Mrs. Tubbs took a step backward. "You're crazy, aren't you?" she asked. "I knew it! I knew it! Every time I meet a nice man, it turns out that he's completely nuts!"

"I'm not crazy, Mrs. Ticks, but we have to go. NOW!"

"There, that will hold them," said Gregor. He and the other two spies stepped back and looked at their handiwork.

Sean and Melissa sat on the roof, back-to-back, tied and gagged. Slobs was tied to a nearby railing.

"What now?" Sergei asked.

Gregor shrugged. "Now we must leave."

"So soon?"

"If the children have found us, others will soon follow," Gregor said. "We must leave at once."

Sergei turned and looked at the kids. "And them?"

"They stay here," Gregor said. "It may be days before anyone finds them . . . if ever." Then, turning to them, he said, "Good luck, children."

Working together, the spies pulled the tarp off the machine. Both Sean's and Melissa's eyes widened. It *was* the *Dragonfly*, the helicopter that had been stolen. They watched helplessly as the men climbed on board the craft and started up the engine.

It puttered and sputtered until it roared to life. Louder and louder it grew until the engine was screaming. And then, ever so slowly, the helicopter lifted off the roof and into the air. It looked like they were going to make a clean getaway until . . .

Suddenly another, much smaller, helicopter appeared over the roof of the building. It immediately moved into position, blocking the *Dragonfly*'s escape.

"Lud Ibn Trib!" Sean said. (At least that's what it sounded like with the gag in his mouth). Translation: "Look! It's Trip!"

He was right! It was Trip! And there was Mrs. Tubbs sitting beside him, green from airsickness!

CLANG!

The two helicopters banged against each other.

Not only was the *Dragonfly* bigger, but it was a lot faster and tougher. If this was going to be an air battle, there was absolutely no way Trip could win.

Then suddenly, to Sean's surprise, Melissa jumped to her feet! Somehow she had gotten free! She ripped the gag out of her brother's mouth and began cutting at the ropes with . . . her ring! The U.S.A. ring their father had given her!

"Some of these rhinestones are pretty sharp," she said as the ropes finally gave way.

"Have I ever told you how much I love that ring?" Sean asked as he scrambled to his feet.

"Me too!" Melissa grinned as she raced to untie Slobs.

Meanwhile, the *Dragonfly* was forced to hover just a few feet above the roof. Every time the pilot made an attempt to fly away, Trip's helicopter blocked him.

Unsure what to do, but knowing he had to do something, Sean ran toward the *Dragonfly*. Then, with a yell, "Augh!" he jumped up, grabbed the cockpit door, and tried to climb inside. The pilot kicked at him, but Sean hung on.

At the same time, Trip was preparing to jump from his helicopter onto the other side of the *Dragonfly*.

"Don't leave me!" Mrs. Tubbs cried, shouting over the noise of the whirling rotors.

"Just hold the throttle like this!" Trip said. "That will keep her steady. I'll be right back!"

Before Mrs. Tubbs could protest, he jumped for the *Dragonfly*. It was close, but he made it! As he climbed inside he pulled a can of tear gas out of his pocket.

"Don't make me use this!" he shouted.

"Get him!" Gregor shouted.

As Gregor's men moved toward him, Trip sprayed the tear gas directly . . .

"OW! COUGH! HACK!"

. . . into his own face!

He dropped the tear-gas canister to the floor, and everyone scrambled for it.

Unfortunately, it was about this time that the frightened Mrs. Tubbs jerked the throttle, causing her helicopter to shoot forward and . . .

KA-BLANG! KA-BOOM!

. . . smash into the *Dragonfly* hard, sending it spinning crazily into a nearby power line. Sparks flew as the line collapsed to the roof below. But not the chopper. It veered to the left and finally took off, high into the sky.

Suddenly a squadron of soldiers swarmed through the stairway door and onto the roof directly beside Melissa and Slobs.

"They're getting away, sir!" one of the men shouted to his captain. "What should we do?"

"Radio the base," the captain ordered. "They'll have to shoot her down."

"No!" Melissa shouted. "That's my brother up there!"

Meanwhile, the *Dragonfly* lifted higher into the sky and started to zoom forward . . . straight toward the Capitol Mall. That's when Sean finally managed to get inside and grab the throttle. But only for a second, until . . .

Gregor pushed him aside and had the throttle!

Then Sergei had the throttle!

Then Sean.

Then Gregor again.

Trip would have liked to join in. But he was too busy stumbling over the tear-gas canister . . . until he stumbled one too many times and went flying out the door!

"Eeeeyow!"

"Trip!" Sean shouted.

"Down here!"

Somehow the secret agent had managed to grab hold of one of the chopper's landing skids. Now he dangled some three hundred feet above the ground, his Abraham Lincoln disguise remarkably staying intact.

Down below, tourists were starting to look up.

"Hey!" one shouted. "Isn't that Abraham Lincoln hanging from that helicopter?"

"Nah," his wife replied. "Probably just his stunt double."

Meanwhile, the *Dragonfly* went up . . .

115

. . . . then down . . .

. . . and up again!

While Trip hung on for dear life!

Suddenly they were coming very close to the capitol dome until Trip's feet . . .

WHACK-WHACK-WHACK
"OW! OW! OW!"

. . . banged across the roof.

Next up was the . . .

KER-WHACK!
"YEEOW!"

. . . Jefferson Memorial.

Then, look out, here comes the Washington Monument!

Whew! That was close, they just missed it. But not the . . .

KER-WHAM!
"OOOOFFFfff . . ."

Lincoln Memorial!

This was getting to be quite an ordeal for poor Mr. Trip. In fact, by the time the *Dragonfly* flew over the White House, he was barely able to hang on.

Then, when the *Dragonfly* swerved sharply to the left, that was all he could take. Trip let go and flew through the air . . .

"AUGHHH . . ."

Meanwhile, inside the White House, a tour group stopped in the Lincoln Bedroom.

"Some people have reported seeing Mr. Lincoln's ghost," the tour guide was saying. "But I've been working here for years, and I can assure you, I've never seen anything—"

At that exact moment, Trip . . .

CRASHed!

. . . through the window and landed facedown in Mr. Lincoln's bed.

Trying to keep her calm, the tour guide admitted, "Of course, there's a first time for everything," before fainting in a heap.

"Aaagggghhh!" the tourists cried. "Let us out of here!"

Meanwhile, back on the *Dragonfly*, the spies had subdued Sean and were now in complete control.

"What should we do with this one?" Sergei asked as he tied Sean's hands behind his back.

"I think we should find out if he can fly without a helicopter," Gregor growled.

While the spies laughed over Gregor's little joke, the helicopter's doors suddenly slammed shut. More suddenly still, a face appeared on the instrument panel.

A *green* face made up of electrical energy.

"Hey, duds, what's down?" it asked. "I'm your vegematic pilot. I'll take under now."

"Jeremiah!" Sean whispered.

Jeremiah gave him a wink and smiled as the chopper banked sharply to the right.

"We're going off course!" Gregor shouted. He grabbed the throttle and turned it sharply, but the *Dragonfly* did not respond.

"Just relax," Jeremiah said. "I've taken over the instruments. This will be a very short flight."

"Who are you? What are you doing!" Gregor shouted.

But Jeremiah didn't answer. He had other things on his mind.

Moments later, Sean looked out the window. What was that down there? He could make out some kind of tower. And high walls. Soon they were close enough where he could read the sign:

Maryland State Prison.

All right! Jeremiah was going to land this thing in the prison exercise yard!

The *Dragonfly* kicked up a swirling cloud of dust as it descended. Soon it touched down, and instantly the helicopter was surrounded by a group of heavily armed federal agents.

"Come out with your hands up!" they ordered.

The spies did as they were told and were quickly taken into custody.

"Thanks, Jeremiah," Sean whispered. "You saved the day!"

"Not yet, I haven't," Jeremiah said. "Look!"

His image faded from the control panel and was replaced with a view of Mrs. Tubbs. She was still holding on tight to the controls of Trip's helicopter, which was spinning crazily out of control. "Super J to the rescue!" Jeremiah's voice shouted.

The control panel blinked once, fizzled twice, and Jeremiah was gone! No doubt to spread his green cheer to Mrs. Tubbs.

Now Sean heard the federal agents speaking among themselves.

"The big guy's coming," they whispered. "The big guy is coming."

And then . . . "Here he is!"

Suddenly all of the men snapped to attention as "the big guy" strode up to the helicopter. He was tall and looked very, very familiar.

"Good work, men!" he exclaimed.

"Thank you, sir," they answered in unison.

Suddenly Sean's mouth dropped open in surprise. Now he remembered where he saw him. "Why, you're . . . you're the guy who tried to give me . . ."

"The tract?" the big guy smiled. "You're right."

He opened his leather jacket to reveal the T-shirt he was wearing underneath. Written across it in big red letters were the words *Real Men Love Jesus!*

"Running the local office of the FBI is my job," he said. "But telling people about God's love—that's my life!"

"But—"

"We know all about your agency," he continued. "Been tracking you since you first arrived. Nice work, kid! You did great!"

He motioned to the prisoners standing in the distance and shouted to his men, "Take 'em away, fellas!"

TUESDAY, 16 : 48 PDST

Back in Midvale, Frieda Smedlap had invited the officers of the Garden Club to her house for an emergency session. She had her speech all written out. The main points were

- Mrs. Tubbs has embarrassed the Garden Club.
- Mrs. Tubbs should be asked to resign as president.
- Mrs. Tubbs should have her membership revoked.

The television set in the background was tuned to the afternoon news as the women gathered around Frieda's kitchen table for coffee.

"I've called this meeting because of Hildagard Tubbs," Frieda said.

"What about Hildagard?" the treasurer asked.

In the background, Rafael Ruelas seemed excited about something.

"Well," Frieda began, "as you know, she went to Washington, and—"

"Just a minute, dear," said the secretary. "We want to hear what they're saying on TV." She stepped across the room to the television and turned up the volume.

Ruelas was shouting, "The local heroes who helped to capture that notorious group of spies were Melissa and Sean Hunter and Hildagard Tubbs!"

"Why, isn't that wonderful!" cried the treasurer.

"How nice of her to capture those spies," said the sergeant at arms. "She's a real hero! Now, what were you saying, Frieda?"

"Who, me? Er . . . ah . . . I was just thinking . . ."

The secretary finished her sentence: ". . . that we should send Hildagard a telegram and tell her how proud we are of her? What a marvelous idea! And we should let her be president for another year."

"Well, I . . ." Frieda sputtered.

"Two years!" said the sergeant at arms.

"But she was . . ."

"I say for life!" said the secretary. "Oh, look, everyone! Frieda is so happy she has tears in her eyes!"

WEDNESDAY, 11:00 EDST

The crowd gathered on the White House lawn was large and enthusiastic. All of the major television networks were there to cover the event.

Sean, Melissa, Trip, Mrs. Tubbs, and, of course, Slobs, sat in chairs behind the president of the United States. Mrs. Tubbs' arm rested in a sling. Trip wore a bandage around his head. But nobody else had a scratch.

Mrs. Tubbs proudly clutched the telegram she had just received from the Midvale Garden Club.

"We are honored to have with us today four heroes . . ." the president began.

"WOOF! WOOF!"

"Excuse me, Slobs," the president continued. "Five heroes . . . who exhibited extraordinary courage in helping to bring this country's enemies to justice."

The crowd applauded in approval. Louder and

louder it grew as everyone stood to their feet.

"Pssst, pssst," someone was shouting. Sean looked down at his digital watch to see Jeremiah grinning away. "Not bad for a day's wok," he said.

"That's *work*," Sean corrected. "Not bad for a day's *work*."

"Whatever," Jeremiah shrugged. "So, what'd we learn?" he asked.

"A ton of things," Sean said, looking out over the clapping crowd.

"Like what?"

"Like there's no such things as ghosts."

Hearing the conversation, Melissa looked over and grinned. Then she added, "And that Mrs. Tubbs isn't such a bad egg."

They glanced over to see Trip reaching out to secretly take her hand.

Sean chuckled. "Apparently you're not the only one who thinks that." Then, spotting the "big guy" standing over by the end of the stage, carefully surveying the crowd, he added, "Oh, and one other thing."

"What's that?" Jeremiah asked.

"Real men love Jesus."

"And women, too," Melissa corrected.

"Yup, and women, too."

The applause continued as brother and sister raised their hands and waved to the crowd while Slobs began to bark. There would be other cases for Bloodhounds, Inc., to solve, and other lessons for Sean and Melissa to learn. But somehow they both knew that this last lesson would be the most important of all. A lesson that they would continue to learn and remember for the rest of their lives. . . .

Real men and real women *do* love Jesus.

By Bill Myers

Children's Series:
Bloodhounds, Inc. — mystery/comedy
McGee and Me! — book and video
The Incredible Worlds of Wally McDoogle — comedy

Teen Series:
Forbidden Doors

Adult Novels:
Blood of Heaven
Threshold
Fire of Heaven
Eli
When the Last Leaf Falls
The Face of God

Nonfiction:
The Dark Side of the Supernatural
Hot Topics, Tough Questions
Faith Encounter
Just Believe It

Picture Books:
Baseball for Breakfast

Around the World With Christian Heroes!

TRAILBLAZER BOOKS give you an adventure story, an introduction to a Christian hero of the past, and a look at a time and place that will fascinate you. Whatever country or time interests you most, chances are there's a TRAILBLAZER BOOK about it. And, each story is told through the eyes of a boy or girl your age. Be sure to travel the globe and go back through time with the TRAILBLAZER BOOKS.

TRAILBLAZER BOOKS by Dave and Neta Jackson

Abandoned on/Wild Frontier – Cartwright
Ambushed in Jaguar Swamp – Grubb
Assassins in the Cathedral – Kivengere
Attack in the Rye Grass – Whitman
The Bandit of Ashley Downs – Muller
The Betrayer's Fortune – Simons
Blinded By the Shining Path – Saune
The Chimney Sweep's Ransom – Wesley
Danger on the Flying Trapeze – Moody
Defeat of the Ghost Riders – Bethune
Drawn By a China Moon – Moon
The Drummer Boy's Battle – Nightingale
Escape From the Slave Traders – Livingstone
The Fate of the Yellow Woodbee – Saint
Flight of the Fugitives – Aylward
The Forty-Acre Swindle – Carver
Gold Miner's Rescue – Jackson
The Hidden Jewel – Carmichael
Hostage on the Nighthawk – Penn

Imprisoned in the Golden City – Judson
Journey to the End of the Earth – Seymore
Kidnapped by River Rats – Booth
Listen for the Whippoorwill – Tubman
Mask of the Wolf Boy – Goforth
The Mayflower Secret – Bradford
The Queen's Smuggler – Tyndale
Quest for the Lost Prince – Morris
Race for the Record – Ridderhof
Risking the Forbidden Game – Cary
Roundup of the Street Rovers – Brace
The Runaway's Revenge – Newton
Shanghaied to China – Taylor
Sinking the Dayspring – Paton
Spy for the Night Riders – Luther
The Thieves of Tyburn Square – Fry
Traitor in the Tower –Bunyan
Trial by Poison – Slessor
The Warrior's Challenge – Zeisberger

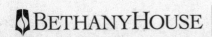

11400 Hampshire Ave S. Minneapolis, MN 55438
(866) 241-6733 www.bethanyhouse.com
Source Code: BOBTB